Look! Look! Look!

by **Nancy Elizabeth Wallace** with **Linda K. Friedlaender**

Illustrated by **Nancy Elizabeth Wallace**

Marshall Cavendish Children

One afternoon, three tiny mice
in their tiny mouse house heard
a loud CLACK! in the people's house.

seff Albers

It was the mail slot. A postcard
addressed to the Bigleys floated down.
It said:

Hi!
Looking at paintings
is wonderful!
Wish you were here!
Love,
Art

The Bigleys
123 Green Crescent Place
Orange, OR 97508

Portrait of Lady Clopton, c. 1600
Artist: Robert Peake
Oil on panel
Yale Center for British Art, New Haven, CT

Well, the Bigleys were not at home, so
the three mice thought they would borrow the
postcard, just to look at it, just for a little while.
They carried it into their tiny mouse house . . .

. . . and propped it up.

"Look!"
said Kiki.

"Look!"
said Alexander.

"Look!"
said Kat.

They looked
from top to bottom,
side to side,
bottom to top.

"I have an idea!" said Kat. She got some paper and cut an opening in one of the pieces. Alexander and Kiki watched, then they cut openings, too.

"Now look," said Kat.
"Look at her face."

"Look through my
viewing frame," said Alexander.
"Look at her hand!"

"Look what I see!" said Kiki. "Jewels!"

"Look here!" said Kat.
"I see **patterns**."

"Me, too!"
said Alexander.

"Look at us!" said Kiki. "We have **patterns** . . . and **colors**, too!"

"**Colors**!" Kiki said again. She picked up a pile of paper. "Put the lady on the floor," she said to Alexander and Kat.

Then Kiki made a fan. She looked at the **colors**. She picked out some ...

…and laid them next to the lady.

"I see
these
colors,"
said Kiki.

"I see
this **color**,"
said Alexander.
"But . . .

"I see these **colors**," said Kat.

. . . I don't see these **colors**."

He got three **colored** markers and handed one to Kiki
and one to Kat. "I see the lady another way," said Alexander.

He picked up the postcard and set it in front of him. Then he went to the easel and started to draw.

Then Kat took her turn.

"Look!" they all squeaked.
"The lady can be **lines**!"

Kat looked at the **lines** she had drawn. "Now I see something else!" She got some green paper. Alexander and Kiki watched Kat cut. They looked at the lady, then started cutting, too.

"**Shapes**!" said Kiki.

"Ta da!" said Kat.

"Ah ha ha!" said Alexander. "I can use the same **shapes** to make this . . .

. . . and this!"

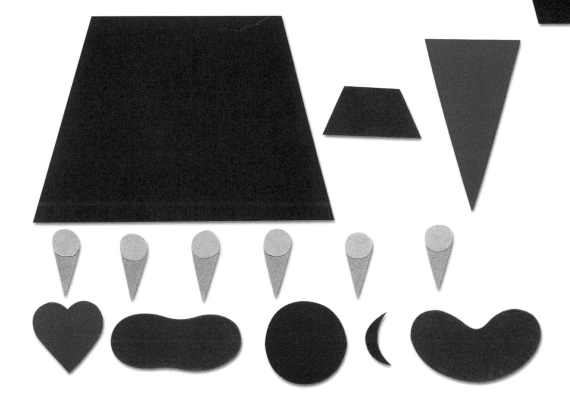

"And this," said Kiki.

"And back to this!" said Kat.

"What if we make Lady Mouseton?" said Kiki.

They got more paper and cut out more **shapes**.

"What if we pick a different background color?" said Kiki.

"What if we add some things?" said Alexander.

"What if we change some things?" said Kat.

Suddenly they heard talking. It was the Bigleys.
"Oh, rats!" said Mr. Bigley. "Where is the key?"
The mice heard Mr. Bigley patting his pockets,
Mrs. Bigley searching in her briefcase,
Betsy Bigley rummaging in her backpack, and
Benjamin Bigley rustling his lunch bag.
There was just enough time to put back the postcard before
the Bigleys found a key, unlocked the door, and came inside.

Now it was
the Bigleys'
turn to ...

Look!

GLOSSARY

Color: Red, yellow, and blue are the three primary, or pure, colors. You can mix them to make all other colors. Colors help us see how one thing is different from another.

Easel: The stand that holds paper, canvas, or cardboard in place so the artist can work.

Line: Lines begin as small marks that can go off in any direction. Lines can be straight ——, curved ⌒, or zigzag ∧∧∧. Lines can be dotted ····· or broken - - - -. They can also be thick ━ or thin ——, dark ━━ or light ——.

Pattern: Colors, shapes, and lines that are repeated.

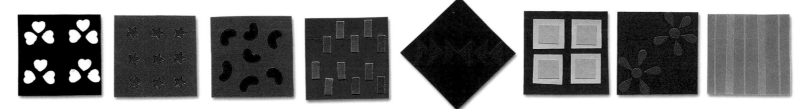

Shape: The form of something that looks flat.

circle

square

triangle

diamond

rectangle

trapezoid

heart

kidney

star

raindrop

cone

crescent

Shapes can also be free-form.

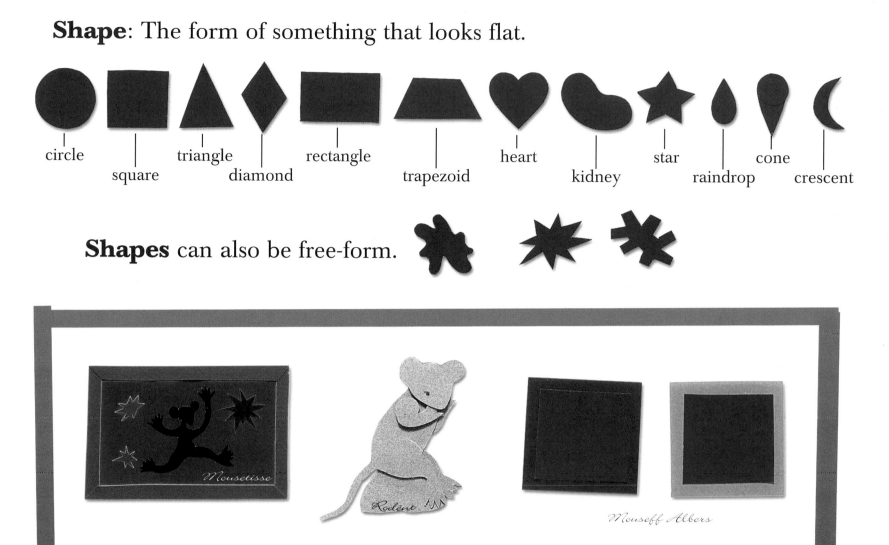

Mousetisse

Rodent

Mouseff Albers

The artwork in the mouse house on page 2 is based on the work of three artists:

Henri Matisse was a painter who also used cut paper to create his art.

Auguste Rodin was a sculptor. One of his most famous sculptures is called *The Thinker*.

Josef Albers was an artist-teacher who studied **color** and **line**.

LOOK AT ME! LOOK WHAT I SEE!
Make a Self-Portrait Postcard

You will need: 8 ½″ x 11″ white card stock (1 sheet makes 4 postcards)
scissors
colored markers, crayons or colored pencils

1) How to make postcards:

Take 1 sheet of card stock.

Fold the card stock in half from top to bottom.

Fold the card stock in half again from side to side.

Carefully cut along the folds with your scissors.

Now you have 4 blank postcards.

2) How to create a self-portrait:

Think about how YOU look.
Is your hair long or short, straight or curly?
Think about your face.
Do you have freckles?
Do you wear glasses?
Think about what you like to wear.

Draw an out**line** picture of YOU
using a marker, crayon or colored pencil.

Use markers, crayons, or colored pencils to:

- Add **colors**.

- Add **shapes** to make **patterns**.

- Add some things to the background.

3) Write on the back:

Turn over your portrait.

Draw a **line** down the middle of the blank side.
Decide to whom you want to send the postcard.

Write your message on the left side.

Dear Uncle Chuck
and Aunt Jane,

This is a portrait
of ME!!

Send me a postcard,
please!

Love,
J.T.

Mr. and Mrs. Gray
19 Blue Sky Lane
Golden Hills, AZ
86336

Write the person's
name,
address,
and zip code
on the right-hand side.

Put a postcard stamp from the post office in the upper right-hand corner.

4) Mail the postcard!

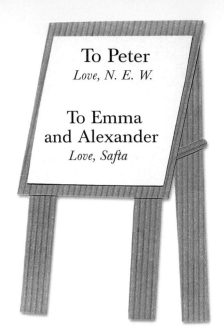

To Peter
Love, N. E. W.

To Emma
and Alexander
Love, Safta

Thanks to the Yale Center for British Art, Paul Mellon Collection, for permission to use
"Portrait of a Woman, traditionally identified as Mary Clopton (born Waldegrave), of Kentwell Hall, Suffolk,"
by Robert Peake, c. 1551–1619, c. 1600, oil on panel, 44³/₄" x 34³/₄" in. (112.0 x 71.0 cm), B1974.3.6.

Text copyright © 2006 by Nancy Elizabeth Wallace
Illustrations copyright © 2006 by Nancy Elizabeth Wallace
All rights reserved
Marshall Cavendish Corporation, 99 White Plains Road, Tarrytown, NY 10591
www.marshallcavendish.us

Library of Congress Cataloging-in-Publication Data
Wallace, Nancy Elizabeth.
Look! look! look! / written by Nancy Elizabeth Wallace with Linda K. Friedlaender ; illustrated by Nancy Elizabeth Wallace.— 1st ed.
p. cm.
Summary: Three mice "borrow" a postcard which is a reproduction of a painting, and from it they learn about color, pattern, line, and shape. Includes instructions for making and sending a postcard.
ISBN-13: 978-0-7614-5282-9
ISBN-10: 0-7614-5282-6
[1. Postcards–Fiction. 2. Art–Fiction. 3. Mice–Fiction.]   I. Friedlaender, Linda, ill. II. Title.
PZ7.W15875Loo 2006
[E]–dc22
2005016934

The text of this book is set in Berthold Baskerville.
The illustrations are rendered using paper, glue sticks, scissors, markers, crayons, and acrylic paint.
Postcard hand lettering by Lizette Boehling
Book design by Virginia Pope
Printed in China
First edition
3 5 6 4

Marshall Cavendish Children